World Above THE Clouds

A Story of a Himalayan Ecosystem

by Ann Whitehead Nagda
Illustrated by Paul Kratter

Soundprints
Where Children Discover...

For my mother—A.W.N.

For my loving family, Tia, Joel, and Marshall. Thanks to my brother, Andy, and to Rod and Darla for their expertise and generosity. Thanks also to the staff at the San Francisco Zoo. A very special thanks to Diane. May the magnificent snow leopard continue to co-exist with the people of this spectacular habitat—P.K.

Published by Soundprints, division of Trudy Corporation, Norwalk, Connecticut.

Art Director: Diane Hinze Kanzler
Book Layout: Scott Findlay; Shields & Partners, Westport, CT
Editor: Judy Gitenstein

First edition 2000
10 9 8 7 6 5 4 3 2 1
Printed in Belgium

Acknowledgments:
    Our thanks to Darla Hillard and Rodney Jackson of the International Snow Leopard Trust for their curatorial review.
     Additional thanks to Joe Fox and Otto Pfister.

Library of Congress Cataloging-in-Publication Data

Nagda, Ann Whitehead,
     World above the clouds: a story of a Himalayan ecosystem / by Ann
Whitehead Nagda; illustrated by Paul Kratter. — 1st ed
        p. cm.
     Summary: A young snow leopard hunts among the other animal inhabitants of her snow-covered home in the Himalayan peaks of northern India.
     ISBN 1-56899-878-3 (hardcover) — ISBN 1-56899-879-1 (pbk.)
     1. Snow leopard—Juvenile fiction. [1. Snow leopard—Fiction.
     2. Leopard—Fiction. 3. Zoology—Himalaya Mountains—Fiction.]   I. Kratter, Paul, ill. II. Title.

PZ10.3.N14 Wo2000
[Fic] — dc21
                                                                                      00-023167
                                                                                      CIP
                                                                                      AC

World Above THE Clouds

A Story of a Himalayan Ecosystem

by Ann Whitehead Nagda

Illustrated by Paul Kratter

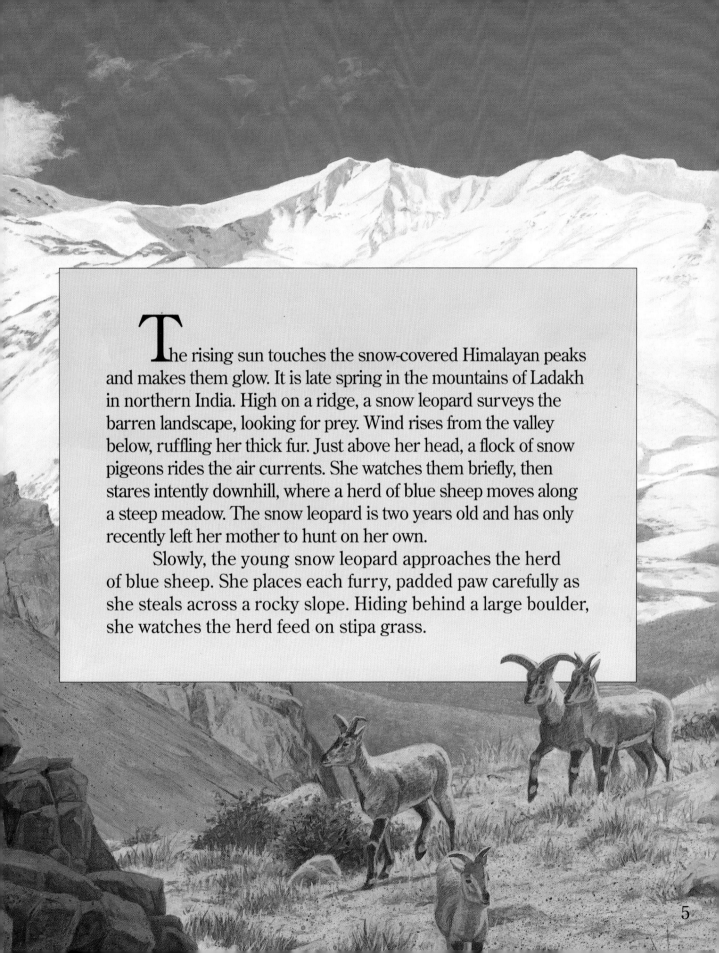

The rising sun touches the snow-covered Himalayan peaks and makes them glow. It is late spring in the mountains of Ladakh in northern India. High on a ridge, a snow leopard surveys the barren landscape, looking for prey. Wind rises from the valley below, ruffling her thick fur. Just above her head, a flock of snow pigeons rides the air currents. She watches them briefly, then stares intently downhill, where a herd of blue sheep moves along a steep meadow. The snow leopard is two years old and has only recently left her mother to hunt on her own.

Slowly, the young snow leopard approaches the herd of blue sheep. She places each furry, padded paw carefully as she steals across a rocky slope. Hiding behind a large boulder, she watches the herd feed on stipa grass.

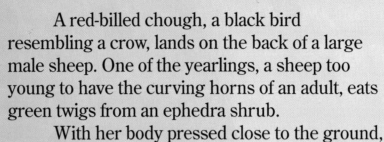

A red-billed chough, a black bird resembling a crow, lands on the back of a large male sheep. One of the yearlings, a sheep too young to have the curving horns of an adult, eats green twigs from an ephedra shrub.

With her body pressed close to the ground, the snow leopard stalks one of the yearlings, then breaks into a run. The frightened sheep races downhill then swerves suddenly. Leaping into the air, the snow leopard thrusts her long tail out to the side, causing her to twist in the new direction. She gets close enough to the yearling to rake its coat with her claws, before it wheels away and escapes with the other sheep onto the cliffs.

The snow leopard sits down and licks her paws. Although she had spent much time following her mother and learning hunting skills, she is not yet an accomplished hunter. She climbs onto a large flat boulder, where, protected by surrounding rocks and partially hidden, she sleeps in the warm sun.

Late in the afternoon, the snow leopard watches a red fox pounce on a vole, which it eats quickly. The red fox leaps again and catches a grasshopper.

Crouching low, the snow leopard stalks the fox. But the fox turns, sees the leopard, and flees. Rather than pursue the fox, the snow leopard waits patiently near a burrow and manages to grab a gray vole in her teeth. It is not much of a meal and she is still hungry.

That evening, by the light of a full moon, the snow leopard walks along the bluff of a river. She hears the call of an eagle owl, then stops to smell a boulder where other leopards have left their scent. Lifting her tail, she sprays the boulder with a combination of scent and urine. Then she scrapes the ground several times with her hind feet. By scraping and scent marking, she lets other snow leopards know she is using this area right now.

At dawn, the hungry snow leopard approaches a village. A woolly hare races to hide among the poplar trees growing nearby. Red-billed choughs hunt for seeds and insects on the flat roofs of village houses, where people store firewood and grain. The snow leopard hears goats bleating and stops by a stone corral, where the goats are kept overnight. When a dog barks, she bounds away to a ridge just above the village.

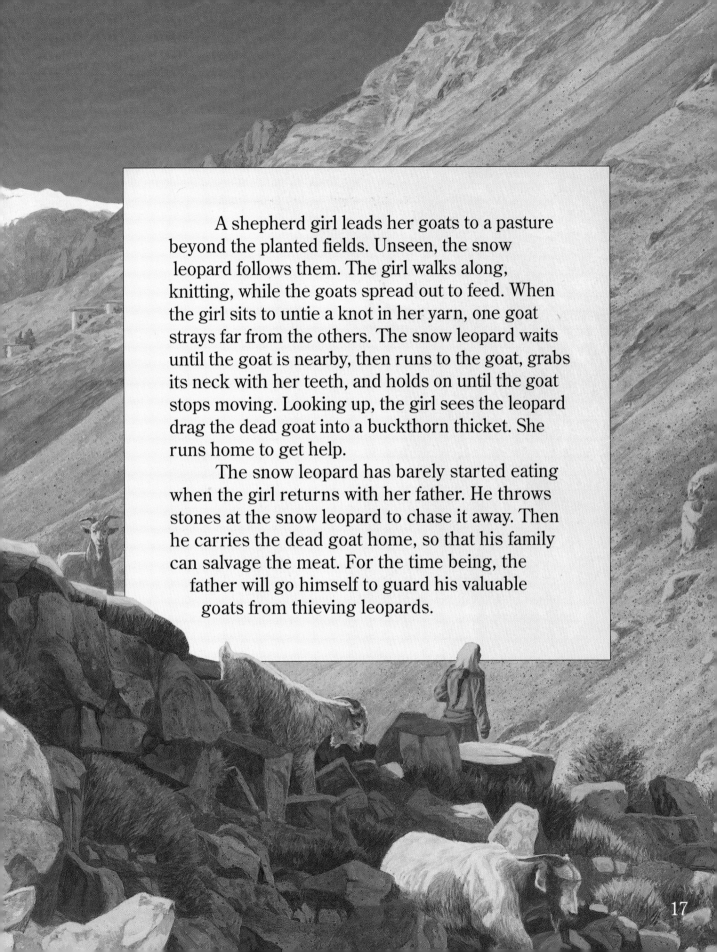

A shepherd girl leads her goats to a pasture beyond the planted fields. Unseen, the snow leopard follows them. The girl walks along, knitting, while the goats spread out to feed. When the girl sits to untie a knot in her yarn, one goat strays far from the others. The snow leopard waits until the goat is nearby, then runs to the goat, grabs its neck with her teeth, and holds on until the goat stops moving. Looking up, the girl sees the leopard drag the dead goat into a buckthorn thicket. She runs home to get help.

The snow leopard has barely started eating when the girl returns with her father. He throws stones at the snow leopard to chase it away. Then he carries the dead goat home, so that his family can salvage the meat. For the time being, the father will go himself to guard his valuable goats from thieving leopards.

17

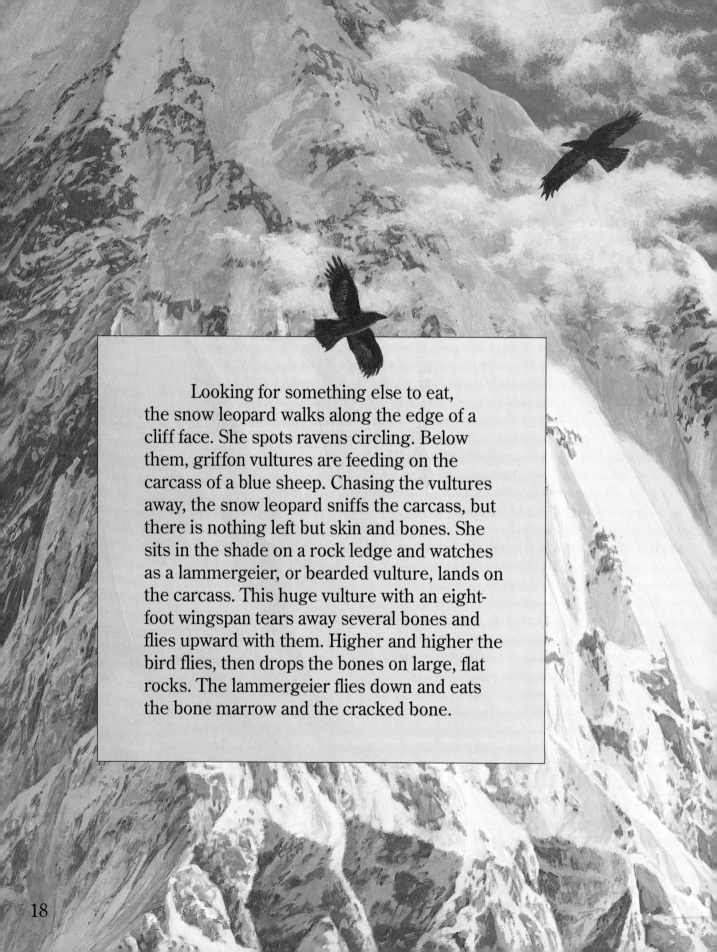

Looking for something else to eat, the snow leopard walks along the edge of a cliff face. She spots ravens circling. Below them, griffon vultures are feeding on the carcass of a blue sheep. Chasing the vultures away, the snow leopard sniffs the carcass, but there is nothing left but skin and bones. She sits in the shade on a rock ledge and watches as a lammergeier, or bearded vulture, lands on the carcass. This huge vulture with an eight-foot wingspan tears away several bones and flies upward with them. Higher and higher the bird flies, then drops the bones on large, flat rocks. The lammergeier flies down and eats the bone marrow and the cracked bone.

At dusk, the snow leopard takes a drink from a stream swollen with water from melting snow. Nearby, on a talus slope, with its jumble of broken rocks and stones, she watches a pika eat yellow-green lichens. A weasel scurries among the rocks and the pika hides. The snow leopard drops into a crouch, her ears pointing forward, and creeps toward the slope. The weasel escapes by diving under a rock.

21

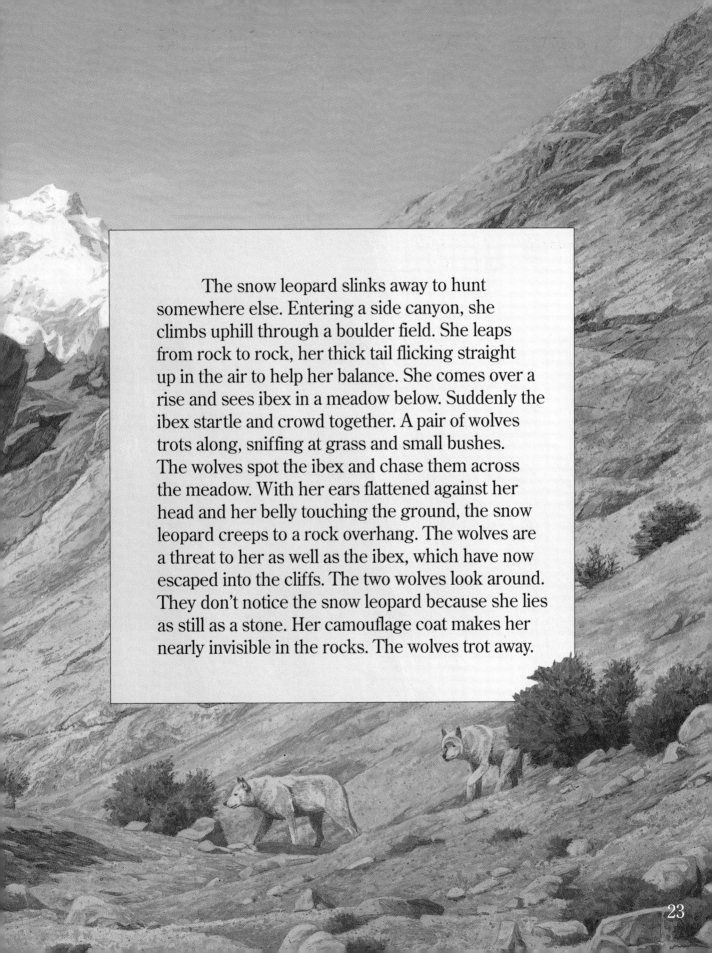

The snow leopard slinks away to hunt somewhere else. Entering a side canyon, she climbs uphill through a boulder field. She leaps from rock to rock, her thick tail flicking straight up in the air to help her balance. She comes over a rise and sees ibex in a meadow below. Suddenly the ibex startle and crowd together. A pair of wolves trots along, sniffing at grass and small bushes. The wolves spot the ibex and chase them across the meadow. With her ears flattened against her head and her belly touching the ground, the snow leopard creeps to a rock overhang. The wolves are a threat to her as well as the ibex, which have now escaped into the cliffs. The two wolves look around. They don't notice the snow leopard because she lies as still as a stone. Her camouflage coat makes her nearly invisible in the rocks. The wolves trot away.

The next day the snow leopard travels to a high meadow. The marmots have come out of hibernation. Some marmots construct new burrows, digging with their front paws and pushing dirt out with their back paws. The marmots aerate the soil when they dig their burrows, which helps the grass in this meadow grow better. Baby marmots wrestle in the grass near the openings to their underground homes.

Using low vegetation as a cover, the snow leopard stalks closer and closer to a marmot dozing in the sun. Just as she is about to spring from her hiding place, a golden eagle flies overhead. Several marmots stand up and give off piercing screams to warn the entire colony of danger. All the marmots disappear into the safety of their burrows.

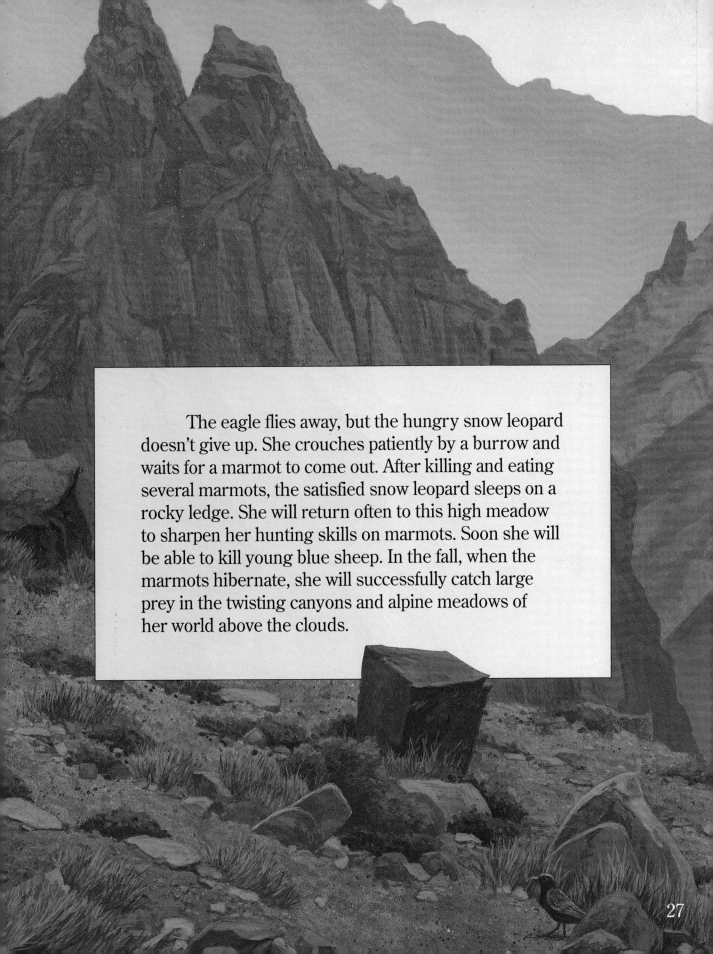

The eagle flies away, but the hungry snow leopard doesn't give up. She crouches patiently by a burrow and waits for a marmot to come out. After killing and eating several marmots, the satisfied snow leopard sleeps on a rocky ledge. She will return often to this high meadow to sharpen her hunting skills on marmots. Soon she will be able to kill young blue sheep. In the fall, when the marmots hibernate, she will successfully catch large prey in the twisting canyons and alpine meadows of her world above the clouds.

Hemis National Park, Ladakh, India

Hemis National Park is located in Ladakh, India's northernmost district. At one time Ladakh was a crossroads on the great Asian trade routes from Tibet, Kashmir, and Chinese Turkistan. Now Ladakh finds itself in border disputes, and the camel caravans no longer travel the ancient silk routes.

About Hemis National Park, Ladakh, India

Hemis National Park is located in the Himalayan mountains of central Ladakh. First established in 1981, the park was made much larger in 1990. The mountains in the park are high, snow-capped, and rugged with elevations ranging from 10,800 feet to 21,000 feet. The annual precipitation is only four inches in Leh, the capital city of Ladakh, although rain and snow increase at higher altitudes. Still, this area is very dry with sparse vegetation. It has cool summers and cold winters, with temperatures well below 0 degrees Fahrenheit. Animals here have undercoats of dense fur and feet adapted to travel through snow and over ice-clad rocks.

Hemis is an important place for studying the snow leopard. Because the Buddhist people who live here do not sanction the killing of wildlife, the wildlife in the park is relatively abundant.

Snow leopards are at the top of the food chain in the high mountains of central Asia. They prey on large animals, which, in turn, rely on plants and insects and microorganisms in the soil. The snow leopard thus becomes a barometer of the health of the ecosystem. If the snow leopard does well, then we know that the high mountain ecosystem is in good shape.

One of the biggest threats to the snow leopard is that it can easily become dependent on killing livestock. Initially, the cat sees no difference between wild animals and domestic livestock, but soon discovers that the villagers' sheep and goats are easy to kill. Losing even one of its animals can be a financial disaster to a poor family, and sometimes they retaliate by killing snow leopards. The International Snow Leopard Trust is having success funding environmentally sustainable small-scale projects for improving animal husbandry (the raising and breeding of animals) and increasing income, in exchange for agreements to conserve snow leopards, their prey, and habitat. Local people agree to better guard their livestock, improve their corrals, and not to claim compensation or retaliate against the snow leopard for killing livestock.

Researchers estimate that between 4,500 and 7,500 snow leopards are left in the wild throughout the Himalayas and other mountains of central Asia. Twelve countries have snow leopards: India, Nepal, China (including Tibet), Bhutan, Pakistan, Afghanistan, Mongolia, Kazakhstan, Kyrgyzstan, Russia, Tajikistan, and Uzbekistan.

The International Snow Leopard Trust has also created an interactive education program for children in snow leopard countries. It centers on a Web of Life poster with a conservation message printed in the local language. You can find out more about the International Snow Leopard Trust on the Internet at the website: www.snowleopard.org.

Glossary

▲ *Domestic goats*

▲ *Griffin vulture*

▲ *Raven*

▲ *Red fox*

▲ *Stipa grass*

▲ *Golden eagle*

▲ *Seabuckthorn*

▲ *Lammergeier*

▲ *Snow leopard*

▲ *Snow pigeon*

▲ *Himalayan marmot*

▲ *Royle's pika*

▲ *Red-billed chough*

▲ *Tibetan woolly hare*

▲ *Royale's high mountain vole*

▲ *Tibetan snow cock*

▲ *Gray wolf*

▲ *Ibex*

▲ *Blue sheep*

▲ *Eurasian eagle owl*

▲ *Himalayan weasel*

▲ *Chukar*

▲ *Ephedra*